Shabbat Shalom, Hey!

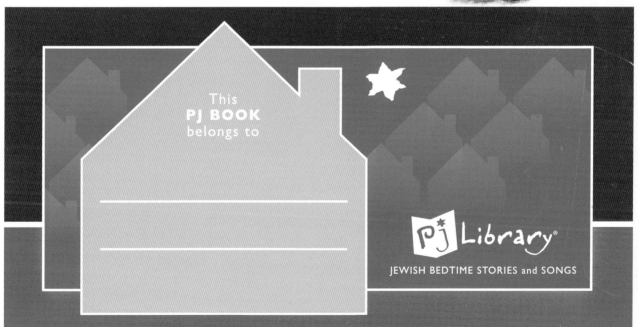

Ann D. Koffsky

KAR-BEN
PUBLISHING

With thanks to my Mom and Dad for giving me the gift of Shabbos

—A.D.K.

KAR-BEN PUBLISHING
A division of Lerner Publishing Group, Inc.
241 First Avenue North
Minneapolis, MN 55401 USA
1-800-4-KARBEN

For reading levels and more information, look up this title at www.karben.com.

Main body text set in Fink Roman.
Typeface provided by House Industries.

Library of Congress Cataloging-in-Publication Data

Koffsky, Ann D., author, illustrator.
    Shabbat shalom, hey! / by Ann D. Koffsky ; illustrated by Ann D. Koffsky.
        pages   cm.
    Summary: On the Sabbath, a lion searches for his animal friends to wish them "Shabbat Shalom!"
    ISBN 978-1-4677-4917-6 (lib. bdg. : alk. paper)
    [1. Salutations—Fiction. 2. Sabbath—Fiction. 3. Judaism—Customs and practices—Fiction. 4. Lions—Fiction. 5. Animals—Fiction.] I. Title.
    PZ7.K81935Sh 2015
    [E]—dc23   2014003668

Manufactured in Hong Kong
1 – PN – 1/1/15

041520K1/B0607

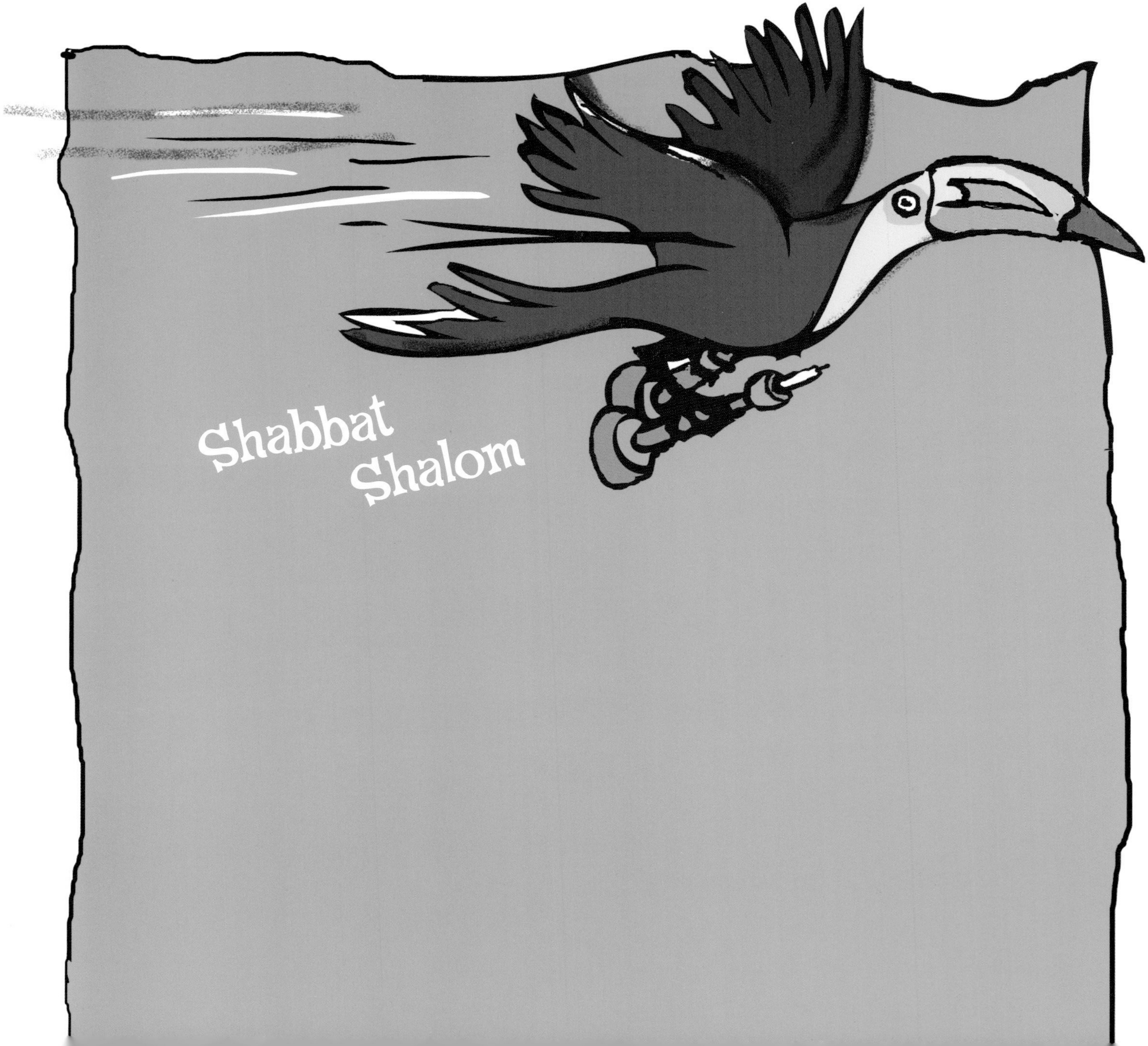
Shabbat
Shalom

Ann D. Koffsky is the author/illustrator of more than 30 Jewish books for children, including *Frogs in the Bed* (Behrman House), *Noah's Swim-A-Thon* (URJ Press) and *Thank You for Me!* (with musician Rich Recht). Her book *My Cousin Tamar Lives in Israel* (URJ Press) was named a Notable Book by the Association of Jewish Libraries. Her artwork has been featured on greeting cards, toys, ketubot, and other products. Ann lives in West Hampstead, New York where she celebrates Shabbat each week with her husband and their three children. You can see more of her work at www.annkoffsky.com.